IGOR'S LAB OF FEAR

LOST SKELETON

by Michael Dahl   illustrated by Igor Šinkovec

STONE ARCH BOOKS
a capstone imprint

Igor's Lab of Fear is published by Stone Arch Books
A Capstone Imprint
1710 Roe Crest Drive, North Mankato, Minnesota 56003
www.mycapstone.com

Cataloging-in-Publication Data
Names: Dahl, Michael, author. | Sinkovec, Igor, illustrator. | Dahl,
Michael.
    Igor's lab of fear.
Title: Lost skeleton / by Michael Dahl ; [illustrator, Igor Sinkovec].
Description: North Mankato, Minnesota : Stone Arch Books, a Capstone
imprint, [2017] | Series: Igor's lab of fear | Summary: Elijah Stapes
wants to be taller, and more like his brother Nico, and friend Cooper,
so he orders a bottle of Tall-Time Tonic from The This For That
Company, which promises to make his bones longer—but he does not
find out where the extra bone comes from until it is too late.
Identifiers: LCCN 2016026565 | ISBN 9781496535290 (library
binding) | ISBN 9781496535337 (eBook PDF)
Subjects: LCSH: Bones—Growth—Juvenile fiction. | Brothers—Juvenile
    fiction. | Horror tales. | CYAC: Horror stories. | Bones—Fiction. |
    Skeleton—Fiction. | LCGFT: Horror fiction.
Classification: LCC PZ7.D15134 Lo 2017 | DDC 813.54 [Fic] —dc23
LC record

ILLUSTRATOR OPENING SPREAD: Andy Catling (pages 4-5)
EDITOR: Abby Colich
DESIGNER: Kristi Carlson

Printed in the United States of America in Stevens Point, Wisconsin.
009621F16

TABLE OF CONTENTS

Go away!

There's no one here!

Only us bloodthirsty ghosts and walking skeletons.

What? It's you?

Come in! Come out of that rain.

I just *knew* there'd be a storm tonight.

I felt it in my **BONES**.

Come sit by the fire and dry off.

Tell me what you've been up to.

Ah, I see you're admiring that little skeleton.

Looks real, doesn't it?

There's quite an interesting story behind that ...

CHAPTER ONE:
THE TONIC

A pair of blue eyes stared through the window at the mailbox.

Elijah Stapes had been staring and standing there for what seemed like hours.

Finally, he saw the mail truck park in front of his house.

He dashed out the front door.

"Any mail?" asked Elijah. "Any mail for Stapes?"

The startled mail carrier shuffled through his bag.

"Just a package," he said.

He pulled out a long, cardboard box.

"Feels hollow," said the man.

Elijah grabbed the package and sprinted into the house.

In his bedroom, Elijah quietly **RIPPED** open the box.

Inside a nest of packing peanuts lay a glass bottle.

Elijah lifted the bottle and read
the label:

THIS FOR THAT'S
TALL-TIME TONIC

CHAPTER TWO:
TALLER

"How much, how much?" Elijah said aloud.

He turned the bottle over until he found the directions.

One spoonful per day.

"That's all?" said Elijah.

One spoonful a day and he was guaranteed longer **BONES**.

Guaranteed to be taller!

Elijah stood up and looked in the mirror on the back of his door.

He was shorter than his younger brother, Nico.

He was shorter than his friend, Cooper too.

If he were taller, maybe people would stop teasing him.

Stop calling him names.

Shrimp. Munchkin.

Pipsqueak.

Elijah uncapped the bottle and **CHUGGED** a mouthful.

It tasted like **chalk**.

Elijah didn't care how it tasted as long as it made his bones grow.

He picked up the paper wrapping from the floor.

THE THIS FOR THAT COMPANY

Such a **WEIRD** name, thought Elijah.

He tossed the paper into his wastebasket.

CHAPTER THREE:
THIS FOR THAT

The next morning, Elijah pulled on his jeans.

They were too short.

He jumped off his bed and punched the air.

"*Yes!*" he crowed.

At breakfast, his father said he looked different somehow.

Nico made fun of his socks.

Elijah said nothing, but simply SMILED.

He was still smiling during his first class.

Then he heard the bad news.

"Did you hear about Cooper?" Elijah's friend Floyd WHISPERED.

"*Something* happened to his legs."

Cooper was the school's quarterback.

"What do you mean?" said Elijah.

"I heard he's in the hospital," said Cody, sitting in front of Floyd.

"They say he can't walk. They say both his legs just wouldn't work when he got out of bed this morning."

"But _how_— ?" Elijah began.

Then the teacher asked them to stop talking, and class began.

CHAPTER FOUR:
MISSING BONES

Elijah and Nico walked home after school in silence, their twin shadows side by side.

Elijah saw his shadow was the same length as his brother's.

But his brother could still outreach him.

Nico had long, **MUSCULAR** arms.

When he got to his room, Elijah stared at the mysterious glass bottle.

What happened to Cooper has nothing to do with me, he told himself. It was an <u>accident</u>.

Elijah looked in the mirror.

He liked the sight of his new, longer legs.

A guy with legs like that would <u>never</u> be called Shrimp.

He uncapped the bottle and swallowed another mouthful.

Cooper had an accident, he repeated.

Then he walked downstairs to dinner.

The following morning, Elijah woke up early.

He rubbed the **SLEEP** from his blue eyes and reached for his jeans.

His legs were still their new length.

But when he pulled on a hoodie, the sleeves were too short.

His arms had grown longer.

"*Yes!*" cried Elijah.

At the same time he heard a
SCREAM.

He ran into his brother's room.

Nico was lying in bed, yelling at
the top of his lungs.

Elijah's father rushed into the
bedroom.

"What's *wrong*?" he asked.

"MY ARMS!" wailed Nico. **"I CAN'T
MOVE MY ARMS!"**

The boy <u>groaned</u> and thrashed on
the bed.

Mr. Stapes knelt and placed a hand on one of Nico's arms.

"NOOOOOO!"

The boy screamed, twisting back and forth.

Mr. Stapes fell back, startled.

"I ... I can't feel the bone in your arm!" he said.

Nico screamed again. Then he passed out.

Mr. Stapes grabbed Elijah's shoulder.

"Quick, son! Call 911!" he yelled.

Elijah ran downstairs to grab his father's phone.

After he made the call, he rushed back to his room and slammed the door.

CHAPTER FIVE:
RETURN POLICY

Elijah punched a second number into his father's phone.

A message **BUZZED** in the boy's ear.

"Thanks for calling **THIS FOR THAT**," said the recorded voice.

"Please leave a message at the tone."

Elijah cried out.

"**TAKE IT BACK!**" he pleaded into the phone. "**I DON'T <u>WANT</u> TO BE TALLER!**"

Elijah thought about his brother's arms.

He remembered that Cooper had gone to the hospital.

"Take it all back!" said Elijah.

"I don't want it anymore!"

The phone **BUZZED** at the other end, and then went dead.

CHAPTER SIX:
TAKING IT ALL BACK

"Elijah!" shouted Mr. Stapes. "Did you call for help?"

He heard no reply.

He reluctantly left Nico's room and walked down the hall.

Mr. Stapes threw open the door to Elijah's bedroom.

Another **SCREAM** filled the house.

This time it came from Mr. Stapes.

On the floor of Elijah's room lay his phone next to a boneless **BLOB** of hair and flesh.

A **BLOB** with blue eyes that stared up at him for help.

The kind people at This for That let me borrow Elijah's skeleton.

I *do* feel sorry for Mr. Stapes, though.

POURING his son into a plastic bag and taking him to the doctor.

All three boys were cursed by Elijah's *one* wish.

It's not that important to be tall, is it?

But it's important to accept yourself. Now that takes <u>real</u> backbone.

Certainly better than *no bones* at all, wouldn't you say?

Hehe. Heh Heh Heh Heh

PROFESSOR IGOR'S LAB NOTES

Oh, you want to learn more about the human skeleton? Why, I'll throw you a bone and tell you little...

Your skeleton is the system of bones in the body. Bones give your body its shape. Bones are connected by joints. Knees and shoulders are joints. Joints allow your body to move. Your backbone, also called a spine, runs down the middle of your back. It allows you to twist and bend.

But how do bones grow? I'm so glad you asked. Arms and legs don't grow out from the center of the bone. They grow longer from the ends of each bone. Areas at the end of long bones, called growth plates, are responsible for growth. Growth plates add tissue at the end of each bone, making it longer and wider. After puberty, you stop growing. The growth plates close up and harden.

How tall a body grows has mostly to do with genetics. This means how tall you are depends a lot on how tall your parents were. Nutrition can also be a factor. Be sure you are getting the right vitamins and minerals, including vitamins A, C, and D, and calcium. Also be sure you are getting enough protein. Or else Professor Igor may have to pay you a visit... Hehe...

GLOSSARY

BACKBONE (BAK-bohn)—a spine; in this story, having a "backbone" means to be strong mentally and emotionally

BLOODTHIRSTY (BLUHD-thuhr-stee)—wanting to cause harm or kill

CHUG (CHUG)—to drink quickly

GENETICS (juh-NET-iks)—the physical traits or conditions passed down from parents to children

GUARANTEE (GARE-an-tee)—to make a promise

HOLLOW (HAWL-oh)—empty on the inside

PUBERTY (PYOO-bur-tee)—the time when a person's body changes from a child's to an adult's

QUARTERBACK (KWOR-tur-bak)—the player in football who runs the offense

RELUCTANT (ree-LUCKT-ent)—to show doubt or unwillingness

THRASH (THRASH)—to move wildly about, often restlessly

TONIC (TAHN-ik)—a substance taken to feel better in some way

DISCUSSION QUESTIONS

1. When Elijah says that what happened to Cooper had nothing to do with him, do you think he knew the medicine might really be to blame? Explain why or why not.

2. If you were Elijah, would you have taken the medicine for a second time? Explain why or why not.

3. How do you think Elijah felt when he walked into his brother's room after he heard the screaming?

WRITING PROMPTS

1. Imagine you work for This for That, the company that made the Tall-Time Tonic that Elijah took. What's another product that your company would make? Explain what it does and how it would work.

2. What's something that you wish you could change about yourself? Write a paragraph explaining why.

3. What happens next in the story? You decide! Write a chapter about what happens to Elijah in the hospital.

AUTHOR BIOGRAPHY

Michael Dahl, the author of the *Library of Doom*, *Dragonblood*, and *Troll Hunters* series, has a long list of things he's afraid of: dark rooms, small rooms, damp rooms (all of which describe his writing area), storms, rabid squirrels, wet paper, raisins, flying in planes (especially taking off, cruising, and landing), and creepy dolls. He hopes that by writing about fear he will eventually be able to overcome his own. So far it isn't working. But he is afraid to stop, so he continues to write. He lives in a haunted house in Minneapolis, Minnesota.

ILLUSTRATOR BIOGRAPHY

Igor Šinkovec was born in Slovenia in 1978. As a kid he dreamt of becoming a truck driver—or failing that, an astronaut. As it turns out, he got stuck behind a drawing board, so sometimes he draws semi trucks and space shuttles. Igor makes his living as an illustrator. Most of his work involves illustrating books for kids. He lives in Ljubljana, Slovenia.